WHAT DO YOU MEME

MARC RICHARD

for best results...

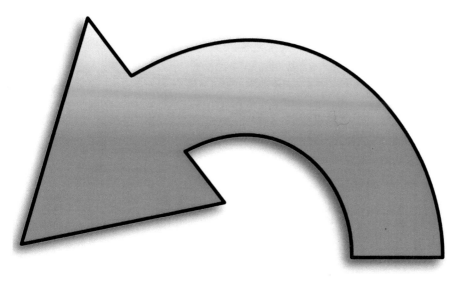

hold book in
dominant hand and
rotate
counter-clockwise
270 degrees.

BAD HATS	GEOGRAPHY	FAMOUS AMPUTEES	FOOD & BEVERAGE	YOU'RE BLEEDING	HIPSTER TATTOOS
$200	$200	$200	$200	$200	$200
$400	$400	$400	$400	$400	$400
$600	$600	$600	$600	$600	$600
$800	$800	$800	$800	$800	$800
$1000	$1000	$1000	$1000	$1000	$1000

GEOGRAPHY

When the ice caps of manic depression melt, what will happen to all the bipolar bears?

I gotta say, not a big fan of Nazis.

Come to find out, I'm based on the British series of the same name.

I just read on a package of jewelry beads "Do not put in mouth or ingest." Then, below in Spanish, "¡ No ponga en la boca o ingerir!" Why the exclamation points when all we get in English is a period?
Is the warning more urgent for Mexicans?

Hey we have the cold weather of the Midwest but we are still southern!

Sorry Tennessee, Nashville is pretty cool, but your state sucks. Plus, you have too many double letters.

CAN WE JUST GET EVERYONE TO MOVE OUT OF OKLAHOMA AND FENCE IT OFF AND JUST LEAVE A PLACE FOR THE TORNADOES TO HANG OUT WITHOUT HURTING ANYONE?

Jeez, I hope your Tigris is better than your Euphrates!

Come to find out

I'm not valid in Alaska and Hawaii

Vietnam bans smoking in public?

Isn't that like Germany banning beer?

A trucker picks up a hitchhiking blonde. "Where ya headed?" he asks. "Wichita," she answers. "Hop in," he says, "but first you have to take off your shoes."

An odd request, she figures, but she does as he asks. The driver looks down at her bare feet. "I thought you said Wichita," he says. She looks at him and smiles. "Nope."

HUH. THIS MORNING I WOKE UP AND REALIZED SOMETHING:

I OWN OREGON.

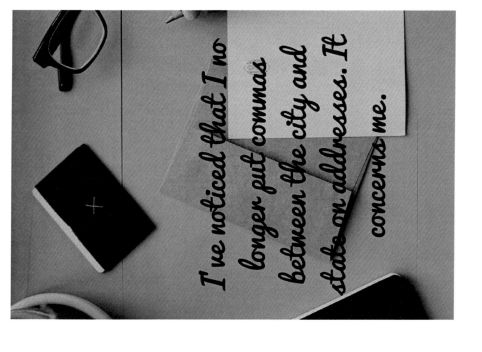

I've noticed that I no longer put commas between the city and state on addresses. It concerns me.

I guess I never really thought about it, but the It's a Small World ride is pretty racist.

Today I feel like that one fat kid in a third world country. You know the one. With the Tim Hardaway jersey.

If Snow was from Jamaica would we have all thought he was an amazing reggae artist? "Informer" was great.

It's because he's Canadian, isn't it?

People say we are all immigrants. I say none of us are. we are all from Pangea. We didn't move. The land did.

AM I THE ONLY AMERICAN WHO THINKS NOTHING OF IT WHEN ONE OF OUR ACTORS CAN PULL OFF A BRITISH ACCENT, BUT IS ASTOUNDED WHEN A BRITISH ACTOR CAN DO AN AMERICAN ONE?

WENT ONTO GOOGLE EARTH TO SEE IF I COULD GET A CLOSEUP OF ANTARCTICA. I NOTICED THAT ALL ACROSS THE CONTINENT, WERE LOGOS SAYING "C. 2016 GOOGLE". DAMN YOU, GOOGLE. NOW YOU'RE DEFACING AN ENTIRE CONTINENT? FOR WHAT? A LITTLE MORE ADVERTISING REVENUE? HOW DID YOU DO IT? CHISEL IT IN THE ICE? THIS DOESN'T DO ONE BIT OF GOOD TO HELP FIGHT GLOBAL WARMING.

Thinking about applying for the Native American run Western Sky loan.

But I have my reservations.

Tennessee...

There's a Portland, Tennessee. What the hell is it the port of? It's a landlocked state. And while we're on the subject, Murfreesboro.

Really? Murfreesboro?

FOOD AND BEVERAGE

The Italian sandwich meat mortadella literally translates into "Meat of the dead".

If people were onions, there would be no war.

Just onions.

Went to McDonald's this morning. She told me to pull up to the last window.

Last window? I understand first window, but last window? Does this mean the window on the door by the front of the building? The window across the street? Or, oh my god, my last window ever? Am I gonna die? I just want my Egg McMuffin.

Discoverer of asparagus: "Hey look what I found in my cabbage patch." "What is it?" "I don't know but it tastes horrible, and if you eat it, your pee smells like you've been fuckin' an actual cabbage patch." "Well, alright just stand there, grill er up."

My favorite thing about horses is the gummy bears.

100% of all the food we eat has been genetically modified from its true original form. Try staying away from GMO's now.

If I opened a pizza shop, I would call it LMNOPizza. You're welcome.

Teach a man to fish, he'll eat for a lifetime.

Teach a fish to man, he'll be confused as fuck.

Box of
Doritos on
our counter.
Says on box:
perfect for
food

I'm going ou
on a limb here
and I'm gonna
say I'm fucking
sick o
pomegranate

Ok, so every time I'm getting coffee (I take it black), and a black person happens to come up and see me getting my coffee, and how I take it, I feel a connection. Like they're thinking, "That's what's up".

Sometimes I cry when I'm chopping carrots because I don't want the onions to get a complex.

Say what you want about Adam Richman, he knows when to quit. I respect that. which is why Andrew Zimmern makes me sick. "Mmm, zebra brain chow mein? Don't mind if I do!"

I used to eat everything on an apple: the core, seeds, stem, and the little fluffy part on the bottom. Then I grew a tree in my belly. It was pretty useful in the not-having-to-buy-apples department, but you should see how I had to pick them.

I like corn muffins, but they're too crumbly. They need to make corn muffin glue.

Why do cinnamon candies taste nothing like cinnamon? You think they could have gotten it somewhat close.

There is no substitute for MSG

If energy levels were measured in chocolate, I would be asparagus.

I think the best thing about being a TV star is all the free chips you get. Like any time you want chips of any flavor, all you have to do is flash your smile and say, "Barbecue, please."

Went to Sbarro for lunch. "I'll have the ziti and meatballs please" for 8.35. "What do you want to drink?" she asks. "I'm all set with the drink," I tell her in my least condescending voice. "Actually it's cheaper with the drink," she says. Cheaper WITH the drink? Ok weird, but I'll just get the drink and throw it away. "Fine then. A Dr. Pepper." I say. "That'll be 9.94," she says. Dumb whore.

I will never tell a bitch to make me a sandwich. I will, however, tell a bitch to take two pieces of bread and put meat and cheese and a condiment of her choice between them, and deliver it to me with a kosher dill spear and a beer.

Just bought a 12-pack variety of beers with 6 mystery beers. Three of which were hefeweizen. You can't just surprise someone with hefeweizen! That's like saying, "Here's a few beers that will migrate to the back of your fridge till you have company you don't really like too much over, if you even remember they're in there."

Why don't tuna cans have sturdier lids?

What's weird is that everybody has at least one soy sauce packet in their fridge.

Back in the '20s you used to give a kid a lollipop, either because you liked the cut of their jib, or you wanted them to scram so you wanted them to scram, so no questions. In the '80s you had to run it by the parents to assure them you weren't a pedophile. Now you have to run it by the parents to make sure the child isn't allergic to gluten.

A sandwich is just a sandwich.

But a sandwich with Miracle Whip has Miracle Whip on it.

Nothing like the smell of a bag of plain chips when you first open them. Smells like potatoes, diesel, and squashed dreams.

I prefer soda in cans and beer in bottles. Who's with me? (Disclaimer: I have since changed my tune about beer. Not soda, though. Although I don't drink much soda nowadays. Mostly I drink water. Am I overexplaining? I think I'm overexplaining.)

One adjective that you never hear regarding mayonnaise:

Refreshing

"Man, you just like a sandwich... inbred."

CHIPOTLE NEEDS TO START CARRYING DESSERT ITEMS.

Thank God for Five Guys Burgers. If there were only four guys, it would suck.

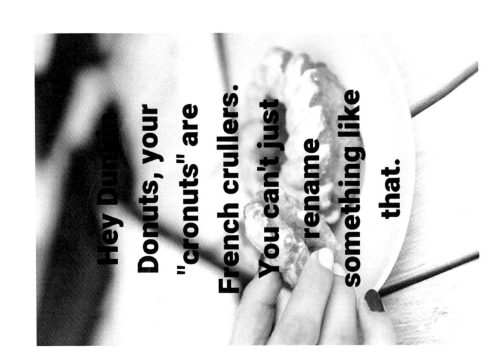

Hey Dunkin Donuts, your "cronuts" are French crullers. You can't just rename something like that.

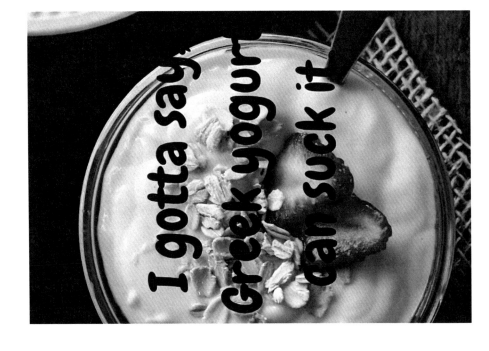

I gotta say, Greek yogurt can suck it

They just found out that ketchup is linked to artery hardening, causing brain dysfunction. Catsup, however, is still ok.

Watermelon is America's worst fruit. Plain and simple.

Anyone that thinks differently is incorrect.

Last time I went to Tim Horton's they were out of donuts.

After quite a while I returned to get one of their not-half-bad breakfast sandwiches and an OJ.

"Sorry sir, we're all out of orange juice. Will apple do? WILL APPLE DO? What am I, five? Or do I seem like the type who enjoys drinking urine-flavored beverages? I'll just get one of your horrible coffees in one of your thin-walled cups. Screw you, Canada.

I have the baked stuffed colostomy.

I prefer peanut M&M's to plain ones. But I spit out the peanuts.

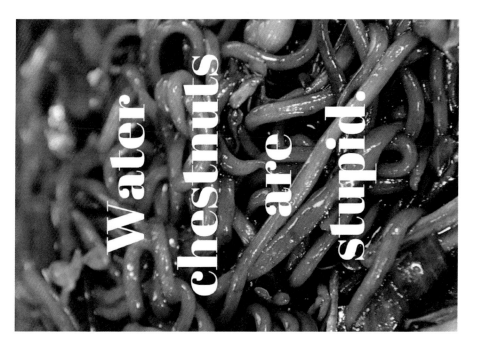

Water chestnuts are stupid.

Hey Cracker Jacks, you can let go of the whole "prize inside" angle. You ain't impressin anybody anymore. You gotta know when to fold 'em.

Ok so I went out and got some KFC. Best part about a night on the town was watching some 14-year-old dressed like Miley Cyrus take a sharpened chicken bone to the neck.

Wasn't me.

There was a time when just the smell of blood would get me excited. Ever since I lost my sense of smell, I have to taste it to get off. It kinda sucks.

The world is a donut and we are but holes.

"Skirt steak" sounds like a euphemism for vagina

I wish chickens laid hard boiled eggs with thousand island dressing on them

I GO TO DUNKIN DONUTS AND ORDER A LARGE BLACK COFFEE, AND THEY ASSUME I WANT IT ICED. ARE YOU KIDDING ME? ICED BLACK COFFEE? NOW I HAVE TO SPECIFY I WANT MY COFFEE HOT? NEXT THING YOU KNOW, THEY'LL ASSUME I ALSO WANT IT DECAF. THANKS A LOT, DECAF ICED COFFEE DRINKERS OF THE WORLD.

If vomit tasted good, I bet people would do it more often.

You'd think that eggs would at least taste a little bit like chicken.

pico is no substitute for salsa.

You forget how good toast and jam is till you have toast and jam.

So word of advice to Dunkin Donuts people #3: If you're out of low-fat milk, and I say whole is fine, and all you can find is chocolate, don't tell me all the rest of the milk has expired. That's not appetizing.

Just say you're out of milk; that's all I need to know.

ME: I'll have a medium black coffee.

DUNKIN DONUTS GUY: Medium black coffee, will there be cream and sugar?

ME: Yes. As long as it starts out black, I don't care what you put in it.

There was a warning on tv last night, to beware of pizza fliers slipped under your hotel door, to not order pizza from them, it was a scam that was going around. I think people got robbed or something. And then I thought, what a great idea for a story. Except in my story, they would kill the people and slaughter them and use them as pizza toppings, so that they could run a legitimate pizza business.

I find it disappointing that the only thing that makes Swedish Fish Swedish is the fact they have the word "Swedish" stamped on them.

Bananas are ok. But does anyone else find themselves forced to eat them in a disinterested way to avoid looking like they're performing fellatio?

"I'm also available in a 100 calorie snack pak."

Cheesecake is a pie and Boston cream pie is a cake. WHO ARE WE FOOLING DAMMIT?

Had a hot date tonight.

Gotta remember not to eat dates when they're fresh out of the oven. Burnt me lip.

Pretzels: The poor man's beef.

What the hell was ever the big deal about eating crust when we were kids? I always ate that shit.

I was... pussy about it.

I got boils on my belly the size of sausages.

Wait. Those ARE sausages.

You can't fool us, Campbell's. We all know your chicken noodle noodles are just spaghetti.

You know how
they say if you
can't pronounce
something on the
label don't eat it?

Same thing goes
for quinoa

You know it's
good clam
chowder when
you bite into
sand

The chicken was raised for cockfighting before it was ever edible meat. So somehow I don't feel bad eating KFC steroid chicken. I feel like I could fight a cock.

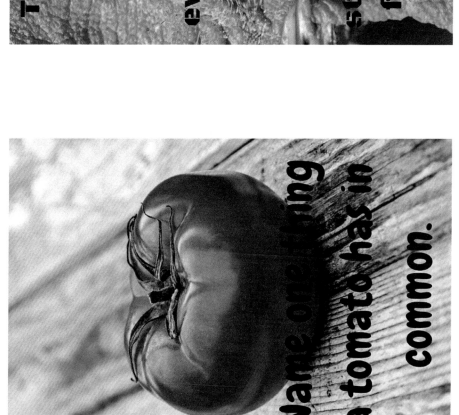

Name one thing a tomato has in common.

When there's a picture on a cookie box of the cookie, and it says "Actual Size", and then I take the cookie out and it has a third dimension to it, I feel ripped off.

put the pepper on the salad
Put the pepper on the salad
put the pepper on the salad
Put the pepper on the salad
put the pepper on the salad
Put the pepper on the salad
put the pepper on the salad
hey hey hey put the pepper on the salad.
hey hey hey put the pepper on the salad.
Put the pepper on the salad.
put the pepper on the salad.

Should I eat gluten free today? Just not in the mood for gluten.

Gelato is the kale of the dessert world.

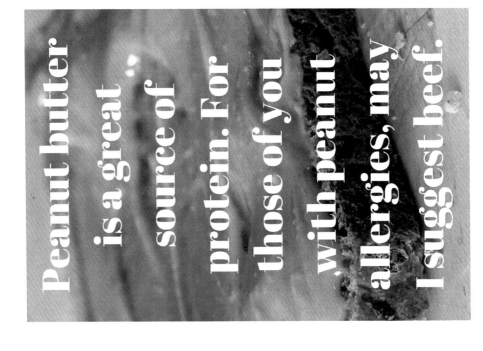

Peanut butter is a great source of protein. For those of you with peanut allergies, may I suggest beef.

I assumed it was...

Saw a whale driving a Prius with a bumper sticker that said EAT MORE KRILL

No one ever looks happy eating a salad.

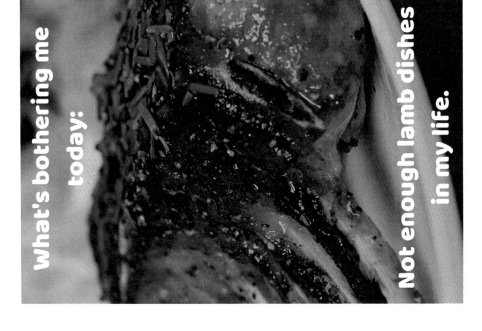

What's bothering me today:

Not enough lamb dishes in my life.

Airline peanuts.

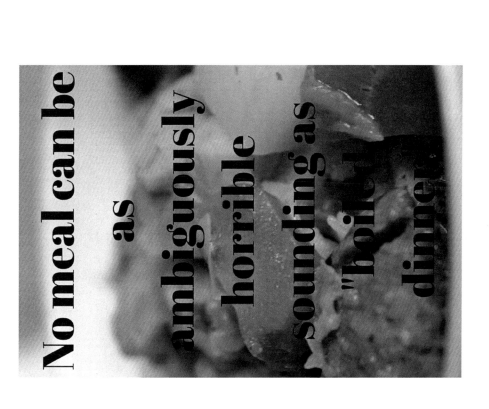

What's the deal?

No meal can be as ambiguously horrible sounding as "boiled dinner"

One of my favorite things to do: eat pad thai. One of my least favorite: eating the leftovers the next day while shitting out the stuff from the night before. Suddenly the 3 spice has become a 5 spice, but the bean sprouts are still BEAN SPROUTS!

She died cause she fucked a pickle and the spices crept into her flesh and formed their own colony, picklizing her.

Stupidest thing I've seen today so far: Written on my package of peanuts: "Produced in a facility that processes peanuts." Thank god all those kids with peanut allergies will now be safe from accidentally eating peanuts that were produced in their own facility.

Sometimes I like to drink soda pop... right out of the can! Take that, bitches!

So usually at burger king I get the double whopper meal. They're running a special, the 2 for 10 buck whopper meal, so I figure why not, I could use the extra bread. The KFC woman hands me two drinks, and my bag not only contains two burgers, but two fries as well. As if to say, here ya go, fatty. This meal is for two people.

I went to an Indian restaurant. American Indian, not Indian Indian. The waiter had on a pilgrim hat. Instead of giving me food, he gave me small pox. Then he quarantined me at a corner table and told me I could do whatever I wanted as long as I didn't mingle with the other customers.

If your last name is Wetzel, you're pretty much limited to running a pretzel stand.

Anyone who likes Pop Tarts more than Toaster Strudel is an asshole. I love Toaster Strudel. Although I can't help but think that the frosting packets look like spent condoms.

These Pods are not edible, guys! However, a little Cascade in the morning coffee can't be beat.

Made in United States
North Haven, CT
06 November 2021